The Movie Star Mystery

By Karl Sturk
Illustrated by Duendes del Sur

SCHOLASTIC INC.
New York Toronto London Auckland Sydney
Mexico City New Delhi Hong Kong Buenos Aires

ISBN-13: 978-0-545-10526-2
ISBN-10: 0-545-10526-9

Designed by Michael Massen

12 11 40 13 14/0

Printed in the U.S.A.
First printing, January 2009

"It's the biggest night of the year!" said the reporter. "The Golden Knight Awards!
"All of your favorite stars are here hoping to win!"
GOLDEN KNIGHT Awards
cde TV

The gang was invited to the show by their friend Glenda Starr.
She was the host of the awards.
“I’m so glad you could make it!” Glenda said.
“So are we!” said Fred.
KNIGHT Awards
KNIGHT Awards

"Look! There's Lyle Glitz and Chase St. John!" said Daphne.

"Like, they're two of the biggest stars around," said Shaggy.

"I wonder if this will be the year Lyle finally wins," said Velma.

"And the one where Chase finally loses," added Fred.

"Are you ready to lose to me again?" Chase asked.

"What makes you think you're going to win this year?" asked Lyle.

"Because I always do," said Chase.

The gang went inside the theater.
A police officer whispered something to Glenda.
"Oh no!" she shouted.

"Someone stole the envelopes with the names of the winners in them!" cried Glenda. "The show will be ruined!"

"We'll get to the bottom of this," Velma said.

"Let's go backstage to look for clues," said Fred.

"Zoinks!" cried Shaggy.
"That's the most food I've ever seen!
We'll catch up with the gang in a minute."

"Roh roy!" Scooby howled.
"You said it, Scoob!" said Shaggy.
"This is how movie stars eat!"

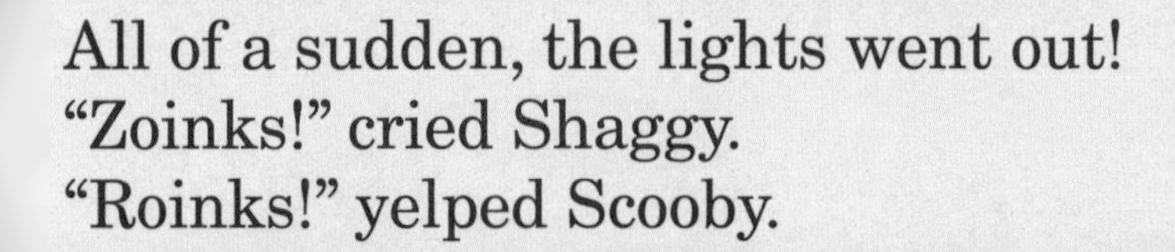

All of a sudden, the lights went out!
"Zoinks!" cried Shaggy.
"Roinks!" yelped Scooby.

It was pitch black in the theater.
Scooby and Shaggy could barely see.
"Like, let's try to find the light switch, good buddy," said Shaggy.
They crept down the hall.

Creeeeaak . . . Creeeeaak . . .
"Shh! What was that?" Shaggy whispered.
They heard footsteps following them.

Shaggy and Scooby found their way to a dressing room.

"Hit the lights, Scoob!"

A masked man appeared!
"I'm going to get you!" he howled.
"Like, let's make a break for it!" Shaggy cried.

Scooby and Shaggy raced down the hall.
The masked man was close behind them.

They ducked into an empty room.
"This is where they kept the envelopes," said Shaggy.

“Wait a minute,” said Shaggy.
“Isn’t this the tie that Chase St. John was wearing? Maybe he’s behind this?”

CLANG! The door slammed shut!

The masked man appeared again!
“Get out of here!” he screamed.

“This is it, Scoob!” Shaggy cried. “We’re goners!”

Suddenly, the door opened.
The lights went back on.
"Oh no!" cried Shaggy.
"Now who's after us?"

"It's us!" said Daphne.
"*Phew!*" Scooby and Shaggy sighed.

“The real question is, who’s this?” said Fred.

Fred yanked away the mask.
"Lyle Glitz!" Glenda cried.
"But why?" asked Velma.

“I’ve been to the Golden Knights a dozen times,” shouted Lyle. “And I’ve never won! It’s not fair!”

"And I would have gotten away with it, too, if it weren't for you meddling kids!" Lyle yelled.

"Looks like we saved the day!" said Velma.

"We'd better hurry," said Daphne. "We don't want to miss the show!"

"Looking sharp, good buddy!" said Shaggy.
"Rank rou! Rank rou! Scooby-Dooby-Doo!"